HAUNTED HOUSEBOAT

Based on the teleplay "Ghoul Fools" by Luke Brookshier, Marc Ceccarelli, and Derek Iversen

Based on the TV series *SpongeBob SquarePants,* created by Stephen Hillenburg, as seen on Nickelodeon

Illustrated by Dave Aikins

A Random House PICTUREBACK® Book

Random House 🏠 New York

created by

Stephen Hillenburg

randomhouse.com/kids

ISBN 978-0-449-81759-9

Printed in the United States of America

10 9 8 7 6 5 4 3 2 1

One blustery day, SpongeBob and Patrick were watching the clouds. "That one looks like Sandy," said SpongeBob. "And that one looks like Mr. Krabs."

"Look at that one!" exclaimed Patrick. "It looks like . . . um . . . a cloud!"
Suddenly, something strange and glowing floated overhead.

"It's a haunted houseboat!" shrieked SpongeBob.
But Patrick wasn't convinced. "Nah, it's probably one of those
fake haunted houses for babies." Patrick marched up the creaky
stairs and went inside. SpongeBob nervously followed him.

"This is sooo not scary," Patrick said as he wandered through the dark house.

But it seemed pretty creepy to SpongeBob: doors squeaked open and then closed by themselves, spiders spun webs, and ghostly hands reached out from the darkness.

With a flash of lightning and a roar of thunder, a ghostly pirate captain appeared.

"Who dares trespass on me haunted houseboat?" he bellowed.

SpongeBob and Patrick cowered. "We do," SpongeBob said. "Why have you come to Bikini Bottom, Mr. Pirate, sir?"

Usually, I come to a town to terrify the people and enslave their souls in eternal torment!" the ghost captain boomed. "But this time, my boat's engine is broken. It needs a new gasket.

"Maybe you two could get a new gasket for the engine?" the ghost captain said. "And to make sure you return, I'll keep your souls for a deposit."
He poured SpongeBob's and Patrick's souls into two old soda bottles.

Then the ghost captain opened his treasure chest and handed SpongeBob a gold doubloon. "This will help you buy a new gasket. If you aren't back in twenty-four hours, your souls will become part of my ghastly crew forever!"

SpongeBob and Patrick ran screaming from the haunted houseboat all the way to the Krusty Krab. They burst through the doors and told Mr. Krabs about the ghost, the broken engine, the gold coin, and the treasure chest.

"Did you say *gold*?" asked Mr. Krabs with a sly smile.

Mr. Krabs marched outside and took a gasket from a car. When he returned, he said, "Let's go see this ghost fella. I'll catch him and take all his gold!"

"Great!" said Sandy. "I've been looking for an excuse to use my newfangled paranormal-critter-detector-catcher gizmo!"

The ghost hunters returned to the creepy old houseboat. They tiptoed across the creaky floors and searched the shadowy rooms. SpongeBob cried, "Look! Gold doubloons!"

Mr. Krabs giggled with joy as he ran to the treasure chest and hugged it. He quickly shoved clawfuls of coins into bags and threw them to Patrick and Squidward.

"Let's get while the getting's good," Mr. Krabs said with a chuckle.

The pirate ghost materialized with a flash of lightning.

"Who dares to take me gold?" he bellowed.

"It's just us," SpongeBob said. "We brought you a gasket for your engine. I was hoping you'd give me and Patrick our souls back now."

"*Arrgh*, a deal is a deal," the ghost captain said. SpongeBob handed the gasket to a ghostly crew member, who floated off to fix the engine.

The ghost captain poured a bottle of orange fluid into
SpongeBob's head. He threw another bottle to Patrick, who dropped
it. The bottle broke, and Patrick quickly started licking up the spill.

"Don't worry," the ghost captain said. "You can't really take a
person's soul. That's just old orange soda."

"I *thought* my soul tasted a little flat," Patrick said.

Meanwhile, Mr. Krabs was trying to sneak away with the gold. As he slowly pulled open a door, it let out a long creak. The ghost captain heard it and swooped after him, shouting, "No one gets away with me gold!"

Suddenly, the door swung all the way open. Mr. Krabs, Squidward, and Patrick were sucked into a strange black emptiness with no up and no down.

"And no one escapes the Void!" the
ghost captain said with an evil laugh.

Back on the houseboat, Sandy jumped into action. "Hey, coffin breath—you'll let my friends out of there if you know what's good for ya!" Energy bolts flew from her ghost catcher and pulled Mr. Krabs, Squidward, and Patrick out of the Void.

On the chest: **Property of F. Dutchman**

As Mr. Krabs and the ghost captain began to fight over the gold, SpongeBob made a discovery.

"Hey, this gold belongs to the Flying Dutchman, the most feared pirate ghost in the sea! His name and phone number are on this chest."

"I was part of his crew," the ghost captain said. "I took his gold a long time ago, but he'll never find me."

Boom! A cannonball crashed through the door and revealed . . . the Flying Dutchman!

"You treacherous sea devils!" he growled. "Give me back me gold, or I'll make you all part of me cursed crew!"

"This might be a good time to leave," SpongeBob whispered. He dragged Mr. Krabs out the door, and his friends followed.

"I wonder how the Dutchman found his gold after all these years,"
Sandy said.

"I couldn't resist my civic duty," SpongeBob said. "You should always
report stolen property to the authorities—especially haunted treasure."